MW00463025

ELIZABETH PEPPER

LOVE CHARMS

The Witches' Almanac, Ltd.

All rights reserved

RITES OF PASSAGE

Love has many forms, many aspects. Three rites of passage performed in witchcraft celebrate the joy and the blessings of love: birth, coming of age, and marriage.

The Gift

The essence of this ritual has been preserved in old fairy tales like *The Sleeping Beauty* and *Cinderella*. We find the theme occurring in both Greek and Nordic myths. The rite is ancient. One that reflects a fine

quality in the human spirit — the wish to impart the best we know to those we love.

The ritual of presentment is both simple and subtle. Circumstances can alter its pattern. Patience and a little improvisation may be needed as the nature of the baby, mother, others present, quality of the atmosphere and mood of the day are factors difficult to predetermine and necessary to consider. These are constants:

1. The baby must be more than three months and less than ten months old.

2. The rite is to be performed within a Waxing Moon.

3. The witch must touch silver to wood just before the gift is given.

4. The gift should be an intangible one.

Intangible? Qualities such as a sense of humor, grace, a kind heart, charm, courage, compassion are favored. An arresting presence, quick wit, great style, natural balance, or perhaps the ability to make the best of any situation might be chosen. Review the possibilities, but avoid deciding beforehand just what your gift will be. Wait until the baby is in your arms and let the higher forces guide your choice.

Establish a rapport with the infant and create around you an aura of warmth and comfort. Clear your mind and deeply concentrate on forming a channel of blessing between the two of you. Instinct will tell you when the moment is right to begin. Wear a silver bracelet or ring. Make sure you're close to a wooden table, chair, or even a door jamb in order to make the contact of silver and wood before gently touching your forefinger to the center of the baby's forehead while saying in a low voice: "I wish upon thee, I wish upon thee, I wish upon thee (the gift)."

The ideal place to perform this old rite would be in the shade of an oak tree. Midsummer would be the perfect time. However, the magic is in the gift and the spirit in which it is given.

The Summoning

On a lonely beach in the mists of early spring, a young woman whose prince has not yet appeared can speed his coming with the help of a witch.

You'll need a small iron pot to hold a fiery coal, the fallen feather of a wild bird, a pure white stone to fit the palm of your hand, a silver cup... and a witch. Actually someone who loves you and sincerely wants your wish to come true; your mother, sister, or best friend can assume the role of the witch. Make sure that the one you choose is not only in sympathy with the proceedings, but able to achieve and sustain deep concentration.

At ebb tide draw a circle in the wet sand of a diameter to match your height. Mark the cardinal points by putting the iron pot with its lighted coal at the South. Thrust the shaft of the feather symbolizing Air at the West. Place the stone representing Earth at the North, and the silver cup filled with Water from the sea at the East. The witch stands in the center of the circle and you, the maiden, at the perimeter. Both face East.

Take time now to collect your thoughts. Center your being by breathing deeply until you feel balanced and sure. Raise your right arm when you are ready to begin.

(*Both turn and face South.*)

WITCH: In the Season of Fire, by the grace of a Young Moon, we meet on hallowed ground to summon the mate of this most cherished child.

MAIDEN: (*Stooping to blow the coal into glowing fire*) I will delight him with fiery thought, surprise him with silence, and brighten all of his days.

WITCH: Even now he comes.

(*Both turn and face West*)

MAIDEN: (*plucking feather from the sand
and tossing it to the wind*) I will honor
him with trust and hold his love as
ightly as the wind does this feather.

WITCH: Even now he comes.

(*Both turn and face North*)

MAIDEN: (*holding the stone in cupped hands*)
I will comfort him with the old
wisdom of the earth while blessing
its continuing cycles.

WITCH: Even now he comes.

(*Both turn and face East*)

MAIDEN: (*Anointing forehead, lips, and heart
with sea water*) : I will love him with
the force, the depth, and the stead-
fastness of the sea.

WITCH: Even now he comes.

MAIDEN: (*Stretch your arms out before you and
then high over your head*)

WITCH: The rite is ended.

Shake the coal from the pot. Pour the remaining water over the coal and cover it with sand. Erase all evidence of the ceremony but keep the white stone as a remembrance of the day.

It's wise to learn the words by heart and practice the procedure beforehand. And once a ritual has begun, under no circumstances interrupt or delay its completion.

Many cultures regard the ocean as a source of wisdom and that sandy stretch of shore where the tides cross back and forth a sacred and magical place. Here you may come to understand ancient truths, determine your fate, or perhaps set in motion the fulfillment of a haunting dream by performing the rite of summoning.

Silent Love

A traditional wedding gift of two small silver plates of about six inches in diameter are accompanied by the following handwritten instructions using the names of the bride and the groom.

A Wedding Rite

Upon these silver plates place fresh fruit. Choose fruit you both enjoy and of a kind easily eaten by hand. Say to one another:

BRIDE: Share fruit with me, be young with me, love with me, wear crowns with me.

GROOM: When I am mad, be mad with me. Be wise with me when I am wise.

From this point on you must observe silence. Make love without words. Express tenderness with your eyes and your touch. The silence you keep makes your love a sacred ceremony, a true and wondrous communion of spirits.

LOVE DEFINED

LET me not to the marriage of true minds
Admit impediments. Love is not love
Which alters when it alteration finds,
Or bends with the remover to remove.
O, no! it is an ever-fixed mark
That looks on tempests and is never shaken;
It is the star to every wandering bark,
Whose worth's unknown, although his height
be taken.
Love's not Time's fool, though rosy lips and cheeks
Within his bending sickle's compass come;
Love alters not with his brief hours and weeks,
But bears it out even to the edge of doom.
If this be error and upon me proved,
I never writ, nor no man ever loved.

Sonnet 116   SHAKESPEARE

Speaking of Love

Love does not consist in gazing at each other but in looking outward together in the same direction.

ANTOINE DE SAINT-EXUPERY

Love is master of the wisest. It is only fools who defy him.

WILLIAM MAKEPEACE THACKERAY

Love sought is good, but given unsought is better.

SHAKESPEARE

Love and smoke are two things which cannot be
concealed.

FRENCH PROVERB

Is it what we love, or how we love that makes love
good?

GEORGE ELIOT

Never seek to tell thy love,
Love that never told can be,
For the gentle wind doth move
Silently, invisibly.

WILLIAM BLAKE

Love consists in this, that two solitudes protect and
touch and greet each other.

RILKE

There has never been a woman yet in the world
who wouldn't have given the top of the milk-jug to
some man, if she had met the right one.

Jane Francisca Elgee, LADY WILDE

The noblest aim in human life is to live in love as
man and wife.

Lyric from Mozart's opera *The Magic Flute*

What you cannot avoid, welcome.

MONTENEGRIN PROVERB

Love is perfect kindness.

AUTHOR UNKNOWN

No cord, nor cable can so forcibly draw, or hold so
fast, as love can do with a twined thread.

ROBERT BURTON

Absence is to love what wind is to fire; it extin-
guishes the small, it enkindles the great.

DEBUSSY-RABUTIN

Pride quits the human heart the moment love
enters it.

THEOPHILE GAUTIER

Those who shun love altogether are as foolish as
those who pursue it too diligently.

EURIPEDES

Love is space and time measured by the heart.

MARCEL PROUST

Delicacy is to love what grace is to beauty.

MME. DE MAINTENON

It is as absurd to pretend that one cannot love the
same woman always, as to pretend that a good
artist needs several violins to execute a piece of
music.

HONORE DE BALZAC

There is no remedy for love but to love more.

HENRY DAVID THOREAU

Casting a Cool Eye on Love

Can there be a love which does not make demands on its object?

CONFUCIUS

Love is the business of the idle.

DIOGENES

All love is vanquished by a succeeding love.

OVID

When love begins to sicken and decay, it useth an enforced ceremony.

SHAKESPEARE

To love but little is in love an infallible means of being beloved.

LA ROCHEFOUCAULD

The magic of our first love is the ignorance that it can never end.

BENJAMIN DISRAELI

One thing is always wrong; to cause suffering in others for the purpose of gratifying one's own pleasure.

LAFCADIO HEARN

Oh, life is a glorious cycle of song,
A medley of extemporanea;
And love is a thing that can never go wrong,
And I am Marie of Roumania.

DOROTHY PARKER

You who seek an end to love, be busy, and you will
be safe.

OVID

The only victory over love is flight.

NAPOLEON I

More wish to be loved by others than to love
others themselves.

NICOLAS CHAMFORT

No disguise can conceal love where it exists,
or long feign it where it is lacking.

LA ROCHEFOUCAULD

If she would reign long, let her scorn her lover.

OVID

Love is the strange bewilderment which overtakes
one person on account of another person.

JAMES THURBER & E.B. WHITE

Love is a traitor who scratches us even when we
want only to play with him.

NINON DE L'ENCLOS

There are people who would never have fallen in
love had they never heard love discussed.

LA ROCHEFOUCAULD

There is nothing in love but what we imagine.

SAINTE-BEUVE

The terror as well as the beauty of love lies in the
fact that it alters all values.

UNA POPE HENNESSY

LOVE AND YOU

There is only one of you in all of time and space.
Only one set of fingerprints and only one voice pattern exist by which you can be identified. Understand
and accept your unique quality. Try to be the very best
you can be within the natural boundaries of ability,
situation, and fate — the hero or heroine of your own
true story.

Before you set out to find a companion with whom
to share life's adventure, you must achieve pride in
your own person. Call on the Four Sacred Elements —
Fire, Earth, Air, Water — to guide your quest to discover

the enchanted circle of spiritual balance, harmony, and the elusive, magical still point of well-being.

Circle of Fire

In privacy and complete darkness, light a candle. Take a deep breath and stand as tall as you can, shoulders back and head high. Hold this posture briefly as you listen to the silence. Face east and raise the candle high above your head for a moment. Bring the flame down to eye-level and hold it there while you turn slowly in a right-hand circle three times. Concentrate your full attention on the blue of the flame as you rotate in place. Raising the candle high again, salute the east as you complete the final circle.

Blow out the flame and in sudden darkness, watch the after-glow rise again and again as you silently wish for an answer or courage or help. Ask only that the outcome of your petition be for the highest good.

Within three hours, three days, or three weeks, you can expect change. Channels will clear in unexpected ways and a different series of patterns will emerge. Some say that by this ceremony we put ourselves in the hands of fate and so ease our tension. Perhaps we relax a rigid mind-set and allow our thoughts to wander as they will.

The Oak Earth Charm

Within the Waxing Moon, go, unobserved if possible, to an old oak tree. Lean back against the trunk with your head, spine, palms of your hands, and heels firmly braced against the rough bark. Breathe in and out gently at a steady rate while you absorb energy from the tree. You'll be able to sense the flow and will instinctively know when to end the ritual. Repeat as often as necessary. And be patient and confident, because our gifts may be blocked but never destroyed.

East Wind, West Wind

From the east comes the veering wind, the one which blows in the same direction as the sun's passage across the sky. A veering wind is purifying. When you feel confused and out of sorts, there is no more effective remedy than a taste of the east wind. Make a ceremony of it. Go to the highest and least obstructed place you know and stand very still facing into the wind. Don't brace yourself against it. Let it flow through you, sweeping away any problems blocking your peace of mind. Ask for the clarity of heart and soul it can give. When you are not clear yourself, you will be of no use to anyone else.

The west wind is called the backing wind because it moves against the course of the sun. It's a supporting wind, one to erase negativity and renew confidence. This is the wind to walk in; to walk at the wind's will. It's a delicious feeling to be borne along by its force. The poet Shelley in his *Ode to the West Wind* wrote, "Drive my dead thoughts over the universe like withered leaves to quicken a new birth!" The familiar Irish salutation: "May the wind be always at your back" is possibly a folk memory of this simple rite.

Blending ritual and nature is a vital key to psychic well-being. By drawing strength and comfort from the veering and backing winds, we prepare ourselves for the work we must do.

Water of Well-Being

Go to the seashore after the tide turns from ebb to flood. Collect from the ninth wave a jar of sea water. The count begins at your discretion. It can be the first wave to touch your feet or a breaking crest you see at a distance. Counting the waves by sight is often confused by contrary currents or eddies, so it is far easier to close your eyes and depend on the sound of each wave as it hits the shore. Scoop up the water from the ninth wave in one fluid motion.

Now stand quietly and draw in the surging energy of the sea and wind. You will sense the right moment to dip water from the jar with your fore, middle, and ring fingers — one at a time in that order — to lightly touch your forehead saying:

> *One for courage*
> *Two for patience*
> *Three for luck*

You can perform this rite on any major sabbat that falls within a Waxing Moon, but it is said to be especially effective at Candlemas. Keep the Sacred Water in a safe and dark place to use throughout the year whenever necessity arises.

QUINTESSENCE

Above and beyond the classical Four Elements of Fire, Earth, Air, and Water is a mysterious quality our ancient philosophers recognized but did not precisely name. Consequently, it became known as the fifth essence — quintessence — from the Latin *quinta*, fifth and *essentia*, essential or that which makes a thing what it is. The word has come to mean an animate power in its highest, most subtle and pure form. *Nous* as the Greeks called the human intellect, World Reason as it relates to Divine Nature, the soul, spirit, ether, the un-

definable, the unknowable all symbolically belong to
the night and the Moon. A ceremonial communion
with the Moon is the way a witch reaches out for that
precious quintessence.

To Draw Down the Moon

At the time of the Full Moon closest to summer
solstice and when the Moon is high, go to an open space
carrying a small bowl of fresh spring water. Position
yourself so as to capture the Moon's reflection in the
bowl. Hold it as steady as you can in both hands for a
slow and silent count to nine. Close your eyes and
while holding the Moon's image in your mind, drink
the water to the last drop.

CREATURE LOVE

You wouldn't be a witch if you didn't love animals. That almost goes without saying. Who knows when it begins? It is as if a link is forged almost before conscious memory — born with the comforting nudge of a cold nose or the recognition of sympathy in a pair of nonhuman eyes. Some say loving animals is a genetic characteristic, while others call it a learned response. It certainly can be encouraged and promoted by example.

From infancy on, the witch child is taught to touch an animal with "love in your hands." The creature's reaction is a living gauge of success. An ability to heal, to comfort, and to truly love develops by means other than speech. In order to establish a firm friendship with an animal, we must learn to use the universal language of the heart which somehow extends human awareness to an incredibly pure and satisfying level. With success come other blessings: the honor of trust, the wish to share, the quiet comfort of mutual respect and devotion.

LOVE LIFE

We must respect ourselves and love our fellow creatures, that's agreed. But above all, we should know and love life. Sara Teasdale, one of America's finest lyric poets, expressed the thought simply and beautifully.

BARTER

LIFE has loveliness to sell,
All beautiful and splendid things,
Blue waves whitened on a cliff,
Soaring fire that sways and sings,
And children's faces looking up
Holding wonder like a cup.

Life has loveliness to sell,
Music like a curve of gold,
Scent of pine trees in the rain,
Eyes that love you, arms that hold,
And for your spirit's still delight,
Holy thoughts that star the night.

Spend all you have for loveliness,
Buy it and never count the cost;
For one white singing hour of peace
Count many a year of strife well lost,
And for a breath of ecstasy
Give all you have been, or could be.

BEWITCHING LOVE

You're attracted. The feeling is strong, compelling. Is it mutual? Only time will tell. Fire charms and the song of the south wind speed you on your way.

To Entice a Lover

At Dark-of-the-Moon when the world is asleep, crumble the dried leaves of the bay laurel tree and scatter them over live coals. As they burn, firm your will and bring the face of the one you desire to your mind's eye. Chant three times:

Laurel leaves burn in fire,
Draw to me my heart's desire.

To Make Love Grow

On a day when the south wind blows, plant a bulb of iris in a new clay pot. As you cover it with earth, thrice repeat the name of the one you wish to be your lover. Water the bulb, nourish it, give it sunlight, and say:

As this root grows
And as its blossom blows,
May my true love's heart be
Gently turned to me.

Potions of Love

Ever since the legendary Tristan and Isolde shared a
love potion, interest in passion-arousing philters has
flourished. Scores of books have been written about
the subject and especially in the world of witches,
recipes handed down from one generation to the next
detail the means by which we may win and secure the
affection of a beloved.

A successful love potion must be attractive to the eye, aromatic, and pleasing to the taste. It should be prepared with great care and presented with delicacy and grace. As we must achieve the right frame of mind to make a wish come true, let the lines of the Roman poet Seneca run through your mind as you concoct the brew:

Love, my darling, and be loved in turn always,
So that at no instant may our mutual love cease...
From sunrise to sunset,
And may the Evening Star gaze upon our love
And the Morning Star too.

Apricot Love Liqueur

Crumble to a powder one handful of the dried leaves of vervain or hemp. Dip seven dried apricots in honey and coat them with the powdered leaves. Steep the fruit in one cup of brandy for a complete Moon cycle. Store in a glass jar with a tight lid and keep in a dark, cool, and secret place. Shake occasionally. Strain three times and serve in tiny liqueur glasses during the Waxing Moon.

Love-Apple Juice

Tomatoes were introduced into Europe from America during the 16th century. For more than a hundred years the majority of Europeans regarded the tomato with suspicion. Its original name, love-apple, suggests an aphrodisiac use. But in this recipe it is the love herb basil rather than the tomato that serves as the magical ingredient.

To two cups of tomato juice add one perfect bay leaf and a heaping tablespoon of the dried leaves of basil crumbled through your fingers. Chill. Make three sunwise circles over the juice, strain, and serve in long-stemmed goblets.

Enchanting Cocoa

Combine three tablespoons each of cocoa and sugar in a small saucepan. Add three tablespoons of cognac and a dash of vanilla extract to form a syrup. Stir clockwise as you pour enough fresh milk to make two cups of cocoa. Heat over a low flame while stirring constantly and concentrating on your intention. Just before the liquid boils, remove from the heat and whip to a froth with an egg beater. Serve at once in red and white mugs.

To Secure Love

This is a romantic version of the knot charm known as the Witches' Ladder. Purchase a yard length of silk cord in a color pleasing to you and symbolic of the love you have in mind. Let your imagination guide you. Do you long for a cool, sweet, and peaceful love or one that's strong, hot and tempestuous?

On the night of a New Moon when you are alone and unobserved, tie nine knots in the silken cord while you visualize the lover you desire. Tie the knots in the order suggested below and say aloud:

Tie one, the charm's begun.
Tie two, no power undo.
Tie three, so shall it be.
Tie four, forever more.
Tie five, the charm's alive.
Tie six, its magic fix.
Tie seven, now under heaven.
Tie eight, work winds of fate.
Tie nine, to my design.

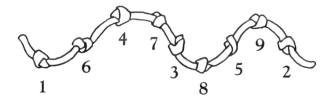

Keep the knot charm hidden away. Should you change your mind and your heart, undo the knots in reverse order as the Moon wanes.

LIGHT OF LOVE

Falling in love is like landing in a strange country without a map. There you are. Lost. You feel oddly elated, charged with excitement, and a little frightened with good reason. Being in love is an awe-inspiring, marvelous, painful, and bewildering experience and yet altogether, a state to be cherished. But out of the wonder of it all, you have to find a route to fulfillment, contentment, or that land of "happily ever after." No easy task, because the road has many pitfalls and one false step may bring disaster. And experience counts for nothing as each individual's journey is completely unique and no two trips are ever exactly the same.

The impulse to love lies buried deep in our subconscious minds and why we love is so complex a question as to make one despair of solving the riddle with reason. Perhaps that is why so many old love charms and spells direct that we seek guidance at love's source — the subconscious mind.

A Medieval Candle Spell

When you feel that you have met your own true love, then take a fat red candle, anoint it with love oil in the manner given, and consult its flame for seven consecutive nights to divine what fate has in store.

Love Oil: Burn three bay leaves to ashes and combine with a pinch each of the dried herbs vervain and basil. Mix the ashes and herbs into three tablespoons of pure olive oil, stirring clockwise, and steep overnight.

The Anointing: Place the red candle on a triangle of clean white linen, its apex and the wick pointing to the north. Using your forefinger, dip the love oil from its vessel and anoint the candle at its center. Lightly spread the oil to the north (wick end) and then back to the base while you slowly and solemnly chant: *I anoint thee in the name of my beloved so that I may know the future of our love.*

The Contemplation: Place the love candle beside your bed and light it just before you are ready to go to sleep. Seek the very center of the flame and concentrate upon it as you say:

Light love's journey
With the glow from thy flame,
Bring me a vision
Of joy or of pain.

Repeat the name of your beloved thrice and continue to gaze at the candle's flame until it seems as if you and it are one. Blow out the candle but hold the memory of its light in your mind's eye as you drift off to sleep. When you wake the next morning, try to recall your dreams and write down all you can remember. Even a fragment or a wisp of feeling is important as a metaphor to be interpreted later when you have completed the seven-night rite.

A Candle for Your Beloved

Once you've found your own true love and an intimate bond is established between you, honor the event by preparing a love candle. There are many versions of the love candle and one of the most attractive comes from a Book of Shadows set down by a New England witch in the 19th century. The tradition is Scotch-Irish.

"Contrive to share a perfect apple with the one you love. From the apple core take nine seeds, seal them in an envelope, and sleep with it beneath your pillow for the first three nights of the waxing moon. If you sleep peacefully and without disturbing dreams, proceed.

"Within daylight hours of the same interval seek a candle and a unique holder for it. The color, form and size of both must please the eye, and, in a subtle way, suggest the qualities of your love. Let your deepest instincts guide your choice.

"On the sixth night of the waxing moon assemble the apple seeds, the candle and holder, a small amount of vegetable oil, a handful of leaves from a birch tree and two small pans. Make certain you can work alone without interruption.

"Draw a small quantity of water and heat it in a pan until just warm. Hold the candle base in the warm water until the wax is soft enough to allow penetration by the sharp end of an apple seed. Press each apple seed into the wax, one by one, until all nine are firmly in place. If the room is cool, continually dip the bottom of the candle in the warm water so that the wax will remain soft enough to receive each seed in turn. While the candle end is still soft, adjust it to fit the candle holder.

"Immerse the birch leaves in gently warmed oil and allow them to steep in the second pan. Ease the candle from the holder and anoint it in the prescribed manner. (Apply birch oil with your forefinger from the center of the candle to wick end and back to the base until the entire surface is lightly coated.) Replace the candle in the holder and hide it away in a cupboard or closet. It must be stored upright and in a dark place.

"Now the candle is ready to be lighted whenever a need arises: if your beloved faces danger or is absent, during misunderstandings, in times of strife or anxiety. Its glow shall serve you well; not only as a comfort, but as an effective safeguard of your love.

"Never allow anyone to light the candle once it has been dedicated as a symbol of your love union. Should this by some ill chance occur, immediately melt out the apple seeds and prepare another candle."

To Make a Wish Come True

With a long thorn prick the symbol of a Crescent Moon in waxing phase in a short, broad candle of pure beeswax. At the noon of night light the candle and with your eyes fixed on the blue of the flame, meditate on your desire as you chant:

> *Gracious Lady Moon,*
> *Ever in my sight,*
> *Kindly grant the boon*
> *I ask of thee tonight.*

In reciting an incantation, remember that the tempo should be far slower than that of ordinary speech. The desired effect is one of quiet emphasis and certain intent.

and if love goes wrong

If we love in vain, lose our love, or perhaps cease to love someone for reasons beyond our control, certain charms can be worked to ease emotional stress. A cool and honest appraisal of the situation and a firm decision to face it as serenely as possible will be magically fortified by a formal ceremony. The rites should be performed as the Moon wanes.

To Banish the Pain of Unrequited Love

Make a fire on a hearth or in a brazier. Crumble the dried leaves of vervain in your major hand as you

concentrate upon your intention. Toss the herb, all at once, on the fire and say:

> *Here is my pain,*
> *Take it and soar,*
> *Depart from me now,*
> *Offend me no more.*

To Ease the Loss of Love

The passage of time and hope for the future can bring peace to a troubled heart. Choose three candles of three different colors and ring the candlesticks with fresh rue or evergreen. At the midnight hour light the candles as you recite this incantation:

By the light of the candles three,
Golden flames reveal to me,
A path, a sign, an omen fair,
To guide me to my destiny.

Gaze on the three flames, each one in turn. An answer may come in the form of an intuitive flash or later the same night in a dream.

To Dismiss Love

Something inside tells you love is gone. Try as you may you can't deny it. Anger, spite and unpleasant scenes can follow. Avoid the bitterness. Turn love into friendship.

At Full Moon snip a foot-long tendril from a weeping willow tree and braid it with equal lengths of bright red and cool green wool yarn. Tie three knots in the braid and hang the charm in an airy room until the moon is in the last quarter. On three successive nights untie the knots one by one in privacy and silence while concentrating on your desire. Before the New Moon rises, burn the red strand to ashes and throw to the winds. Coil the willow and green wool together and place in an envelope for safe-keeping.

LOVE'S SECRETS

As love and magic are akin, we can successfully borrow the Rules of the Magus according to Eliphas Levi, the renowned ceremonial magician:

TO KNOW

TO DARE   TO WILL

TO KEEP SILENCE

Never lose your mystery and above all, remember:

Smile, Witch. Laugh, Witch.
Take your powers back, Witch.

The text of this book was set in Goudy, a typeface created by the American type designer Frederic W. Goudy in 1915. It was composed and prepared on a Macintosh computer. Graphics are from the work of book illustrators Aubrey Beardsley, Margaret Evans Price, Arthur Rackham as well as woodcuts and drawings made by unknown artists of the 15th, 16th, and 19th centuries.